VITTORIA
Book 3

By
GEORGE MEREDITH

Vittoria
Book 3

by **George Meredith**

Copyright © 2023

ISBN: 978-93-57484-93-0

Published by

DOUBLE 9 BOOKS

2/13-B, Ansari Road, Daryaganj
New Delhi – 110002
info@double9books.com
www.double9books.com
Tel. 011-40042856

ABOUT THE AUTHOR

George Meredith OM (February 12, 1828-May 18, 1909) was born in Portsmouth, United Kingdom. He was an English poet, writer, and author, whose books are noted for their intelligence, extraordinary dialogues, and aphoristic way of writing. Meredith's books are also recognised for psychological studies of character and a highly subjective perspective on life that is a long way ahead of its time, considering women are equals to men in all streams. His most popular works are The Ordeal of Richard Feverel (1859) and The Egoist (1879). He was nominated for the Nobel Prize in Literature seven times.

CONTENTS

CHAPTER XIV
AT THE MAESTRO'S DOOR...7

CHAPTER XV
AMMIANI THROUGH THE MIDNIGHT..21

CHAPTER XVI
COUNTESS AMMIANI 33

CHAPTER XVII
IN THE PIAZZA D'ARMI 40

CHAPTER XVIII
THE NIGHT OF THE FIFTEENTH...48

CHAPTER XIX
THE PRIMA DONNA 55

CHAPTER XIV
AT THE MAESTRO'S DOOR

The house of the Maestro Rocco Ricci turned off the Borgo della Stella. Carlo Ammiani conducted Vittoria to the maestro's door. They conversed very little on the way.

'You are a good swordsman?' she asked him abruptly.

'I have as much skill as belongs to a perfect intimacy with the weapon,' he answered.

'Your father was a soldier, Signor Carlo.'

'He was a General officer in what he believed to be the army of Italy. We used to fence together every day for two hours.'

'I love the fathers who do that,' said Vittoria.

After such speaking Ammiani was not capable of the attempt to preach peace and safety to her. He postponed it to the next minute and the next.

Vittoria's spirit was in one of those angry knots which are half of the intellect, half of the will, and are much under the domination of one or other of the passions in the ascendant. She was resolved to go forward; she felt justified in going forward; but the divine afflatus of enthusiasm buoyed her no longer, and she required the support of all that accuracy of insight and that senseless stubbornness which there might be in her nature. The feeling that it was she to whom it was given to lift the torch and plant the standard of Italy, had swept her as through the strings of a harp. Laura, and the horrible little bronze butterfly, and the 'Sei sospetta,' now made her duty seem dry and miserably fleshless, imaging itself to her as if a skeleton had been told to arise and walk: — say, the thing obeys, and fills a ghastly distension of men's eyelids for a space, and again lies down, and men get their breath: but who is the rosier for it? where is the glory of it? what is the good? This Milan, and Verona, Padua, Vicenza, Brescia, Venice, Florence, the whole Venetian, Tuscan, and Lombardic lands, down to far Sicily, and that Rome which always lay under the crown of a dead sunset in her idea—they too might rise; but she thought of them as skeletons likewise. Even the shadowy vision of Italy Free had no bloom on it, and stood fronting the blown trumpets of resurrection Lazarus-like.

At these moments young hearts, though full of sap and fire, cannot do common nursing labour for the little suckling sentiments and hopes, the dreams, the languors and the energies hanging about them for nourishment. Vittoria's horizon was within five feet of her. She saw neither splendid earth nor ancient heaven; nothing save a breach to be stepped over in defiance of foes and (what was harder to brave) of friends. Some wayward activity of old associations set her humming a quaint English tune, by which she was brought to her consciousness.

'Dear friend,' she said, becoming aware that there might be a more troubled depth in Ammiani's absence of speech than in her own.

'Yes?' said he, quickly, as for a sentence to follow. None came, and he continued, 'The Signora Laura is also your friend.'

She rejoined coldly, 'I am not thinking of her.'

Vittoria had tried to utter what might be a word of comfort for him, and she found she had not a thought or an emotion. Here she differed from Laura, who, if the mood to heal a favourite's little sore at any season came upon her, would shower out lively tendernesses and all cajoleries possible to the tongue of woman. Yet the irritation of action narrowed Laura more than it did Vittoria; fevered her and distracted her sympathies. Being herself a plaything at the time, she could easily play a part for others. Vittoria had not grown, probably never would grow, to be so plastic off the stage. She was stringing her hand to strike a blow as men strike, and women when they do that cannot be quite feminine.

'How dull the streets are,' she remarked.

'They are, just now,' said Ammiani, thinking of them on the night to come convulsed with strife, and of her, tossed perhaps like a weed along the torrent of bloody deluge waters. Her step was so firm, her face so assured, that he could not fancy she realized any prospect of the sort, and it filled him with pity and a wretched quailing.

If I speak now I shall be talking like a coward, he said to himself: and he was happily too prudent to talk to her in that strain. So he said nothing of peace and safety. She was almost at liberty to believe that he approved the wisdom of her resolution. At the maestro's door she thanked him for his escort, and begged for it further within an hour. 'And do bring me some chocolate.' She struck her teeth together champing in a pretty hunger for it. 'I have no chocolate in my pocket, and I hardly know myself.'

'What will your Signor Antonio say?'

Vittoria filliped her fingers. 'His rule is over, and he is my slave: I am not his. I will not eat much; but some some I must have.'

Ammiani laughed and promised to obtain it. 'That is, if there's any to be had.'

'Break open doors to get it for me,' she said, stamping with fun to inspirit him.

No sooner was she standing alone, than her elbow was gently plucked at on the other side: a voice was sibilating: 'S-s-signorina.' She allowed herself to be drawn out of the light of the open doorway, having no suspicion and no fear. 'Signorina, here is chocolate.' She beheld two hands in cup-shape, surcharged with packets of Turin chocolate.

'Lugi, it is you?'

The Motterone spy screwed his eyelids to an expression of the shrewdest secrecy.

'Hist! signorina. Take some. You shall have all, but wait: — by-and-by. Aha! you look at my eyes as you did on the Monterone, because one of them takes the shoulder-view; but, the truth is, my father was a contrabandist, and had his eye in his ear when the frontier guard sent a bullet through his back, cotton-bags and cutleries, and all! I inherit from him, and have been wry-eyed ever since. How does that touch a man's honesty, signorina? Not at all. Don't even suspect that you won't appreciate Luigi by-and-by. So, you won't ask me a word, signorina, but up you go to the maestro: — signorina, I swear I am your faithful servant — up to the maestro, and down first. Come down first not last: — first. Let the other one come down after you;

and you come down first. Leave her behind, la Lazzeruola; and here,' Luigi displayed a black veil, the common head-dress of the Milanese women, and twisted his fingers round and round on his forehead to personate the horns of the veil; 'take it, signorina; you know how to wear it. Luigi and the saints watch over you.' Vittoria found herself left in possession of the veil and a packet of chocolate.

'If I am watched over by the saints and Luigi,' she thought, and bit at the chocolate.

When the door had closed upon her, Luigi resumed his station near it, warily casting his glances along the house-fronts, and moving his springy little legs like a heath-cock alert. They carried him sharp to an opposite corner of the street at a noise of some one running exposed to all eyes right down the middle of the road, straight to the house: in which foolish person he discerned Beppo, all of whose proceedings Luigi observed and commented on from the safe obscurity under eaves and starlight, while Beppo was in the light of the lamps. 'You thunder at the door, my Beppo. You are a fire-balloon: you are going to burn yourself up with what you carry. You think you can do something, because you read books and frequent the talking theatres—fourteen syllables to a word. Mother of heaven! will you never learn anything from natural intelligence? There you are, in at the door. And now you will disturb the signorina, and you will do nothing but make la Lazzeruola's ears lively. Bounce! you are up the stairs. Bounce! you are on the landing. Thrum! you drum at the door, and they are singing; they don't hear you. And now you're meek as a mouse. That's it—if you don't hit the mark when you go like a bullet, you 're stupid as lead. And they call you a clever fellow! Luigi's day is to come. When all have paid him all round, they will acknowledge Luigi's worth. You are honest enough, my Beppo; but you might as well be a countryman. You are the signorina's servant, but I know the turnings, said the rat to the cavaliere weazel.'

In a few minutes Beppo stepped from the house, and flung himself with his back against the lintel of the doorway.

'That looks like determination to stop on guard,' said Luigi.

He knew the exact feeling expressed by it, when one has come violently on an errand and has done no good.

'A flea, my feathery lad, will set you flying again.'

As it was imperative in Luigi's schemes that Beppo should be set flying again, he slipped away stealthily, and sped fast into the neighbouring Corso, where a light English closed carriage, drawn by a pair of the island horses, moved at a slow pace. Two men were on the driver's seat, one of whom Luigi hailed to come down then he laid a strip of paper on his knee, and after thumping on the side of his nose to get a notion of English-Italian, he wrote with a pencil, dancing upon one leg all the while for a balance: —

'Come, Beppo, daughter sake, now, at once, immediate, Beppo, signor.'

'That's to the very extremity how the little signora Inglese would write,' said Luigi; yet cogitating profoundly in a dubitative twinkle of a second as to whether it might not be the English habit to wind up a hasty missive with an expediting oath. He had heard the oath of emphasis in that island: but he decided to let it go as it stood. The man he had summoned was directed to take it straightway and deliver it to one who would be found at the house-door of the Maestro Rocco Ricci.

'Thus, like a drunken sentinel,' said Luigi, folding his arms, crossing his legs, and leaning back. 'Forward, Matteo, my cherub.'

'All goes right?' the coachman addressed Luigi.

'As honey, as butter, as a mulberry leaf with a score of worms on it! The wine and the bread and the cream-cheeses are inside, my dainty one, are they? She must not starve, nor must I. Are our hampers fastened out side? Good. We shall be among the Germans in a day and a night. I 've got the route, and I pronounce the name of the chateau very perfectly— "Schloss Sonnenberg." Do that if you can.'

The unpractised Italian coachman declined to attempt it. He and Luigi compared time by their watches. In three-quarters of an hour he was to be within hail of the maestro's house. Thither Luigi quietly returned.

Beppo's place there was vacant.

'That's better than a draught of Asti,' said Luigi.

The lighted windows of the maestro's house, and the piano striking corrective notes, assured him that the special rehearsal was still going on; and as he might now calculate on two or three minutes to spare, he threw back his coat-collar, lifted his head, and distended his chest, apparently to chime in with the singing, but simply to listen to it. For him, it was imperative that he should act the thing, in order to apprehend and appreciate it.

A hurried footing told of the approach of one whom he expected.

'Luigi!'

'Here, padrone.'

'You have the chocolate?'

'Signor Antonio, I have deposited it in the carriage.'

'She is in up there?'

'I beheld her entering.'

'Good; that is fixed fact.' The Signor Antonio drove at his moustache right and left. 'I give you, see, Italian money and German money: German money in paper; and a paper written out by me to explain the value of the German paper-money. Silence, engine that you are, and not a man! I am preventive of stupidity, I am? Do I not know that, hein? Am I in need of the acclamation of you, my friend? On to the Chateau Sonnenberg:— drive on, drive on, and one who stops you, you drive over him: the gendarmes in white will peruse this paper, if there is any question, and will pass you and the cage, bowing; you hear? It is a pass; the military pass you when you show this paper. My good friend, Captain Weisspriess, on the staff of General Pierson, gives it, signed, and it is effectual. But you lose not the paper: put it away with the paper-money, quite safe. For yourself, this is half your pay—I give you napoleons; ten. Count. And now— once at the Chateau Sonnenberg, I repeat, you leave her in charge of two persons, one a woman, at the gate, and then back—frrrrr..'

Antonio-Pericles smacked on the flat of his hand, and sounded a rapid course of wheels.

'Back, and drop not a crumb upon the road. You have your map. It is, after Roveredo, straight up the Adige, by Bolzano . . . say "Botzen."'

'"Botz,"' said Luigi, submissively.

'"Botz"—"Botz"—ass! fool! double idiot! "Botzon!"' Antonio-Pericles corrected him furiously, exclaiming to the sovereign skies, 'Though I pay for brains, can I get them! No. But make a fiasco, Luigi, and not a second ten for you, my friend: and away, out of my sight, show yourself no more!'

Luigi humbly said that he was not the instrument of a fiasco.

Half spurning him, Antonio-Pericles snarled an end both to his advices and his prophetic disgust of the miserable tools furnished unto masterly minds upon this earth. He paced forward and back, murmuring in French, 'Mon Dieu! was there ever such a folly as in the head of this girl? It is her occasion: — Shall I be a Star? Shall I be a Cinder? It is tomorrow night her moment of Birth! No; she prefers to be extinguished. For what? For this thing she calls her country. It is infamous. Yes, vile little cheat! But, do you know Antonio-Pericles? Not yet. I will nourish you, I will imprison you: I will have you tortured by love, by the very devil of love, by the red-hot pincers of love, till you scream. a music, and die to melt him with your voice, and kick your country to the gutter, and know your Italy for a birthplace and a cradle of Song, and no more, and enough! Bah!'

Having thus delivered himself of the effervescence of his internal agitation, he turned sharply round upon Luigi, with a military stamp of the foot and shout of the man's name.

'It is love she wants,' Antonio-Pericles resumed his savage soliloquy. 'She wants to be kindled on fire. Too much Government of brain; not sufficient Insurrection of heart! There it is. There it lies. But, little fool! you shall find people with arms and shots and cannon running all up and down your body, firing and crying out "Victory for Love!" till you are beaten, till you gasp "Love! love! love!" and then comes a beatific — oh! a heaven and a hell to your voice. I will pay,' the excited connoisseur pursued more deliberately: 'I will pay half my fortune to bring this about. I am fortified, for I know such a voice was sent to be sublime.' He exclaimed in an ecstasy: 'It opens the skies!' and immediately appended: 'It is destined to suffocate the theatres!'

Pausing as before a splendid vision: 'Money — let it go like dust! I have an object. Sandra Belloni — you stupid Vittoria Campa! — I have millions and the whole Austrian Government to back me, and you to be wilful, little rebel! I could laugh. It is only Love you want. Your voice is now in a marble chamber. I will put it in a palace of cedarwood. This Ammiani I let visit you in the hope that he would touch you.

Bah! he is a patriot—not a man! He cannot make you wince and pine, and be cold and be hot, and—Bah! I give a chance to some one else who is not a patriot. He has done mischief with the inflammable little Anna von Lenkenstein—I know it. Your proper lovers, you women, are the broad, the business lovers, and Weisspriess is your man.'

Antonio-Pericles glanced up at the maestro's windows. 'Hark! it is her voice,' he said, and drew up his clenched fists with rage, as if pumping. 'Cold as ice! Not a flaw. She is a lantern with no light in it—crystal, if you like. Hark now at Irma, the stork-neck. Aie! what a long way it is from your throat to your head, Mademoiselle Irma! You were reared upon lemons. The split hair of your mural crown is not thinner than that voice of yours. It is a mockery to hear you; but you are good enough for the people, my dear, and you do work, running up and down that ladder of wires between your throat and your head;—you work, it is true, you puss! sleek as a puss, bony as a puss, musical as a puss. But you are good enough for the people. Hola!'

This exclamation was addressed to a cavalier who was dismounting from his horse about fifty yards down the street, and who, giving the reins to a mounted servant, advanced to meet the Signor Antonio.

'It is you, Herr Captain von Weisspriess!'

'When he makes an appointment you see him, as a rule, my dear Pericles,' returned the captain.

'You are out of uniform—good. We will go up. Remember, you are a connoisseur, from Bonn—from Berlin—from Leipsic: not of the K.K. army! Abjure it, or you make no way with this mad thing. You shall see her and hear her, and judge if she is worth your visit to Schloss Sonnenberg and a short siege. Good: we go aloft. You bow to the maestro respectfully twice, as in duty; then a third time, as from a whisper of your soul. Vanitas, vanitatis! You speak of the 'UT de poitrine.' You remark: "Albrechtsberger has said——," and you slap your head and stop. They think, "He is polite, and will not quote a German authority to us": and they think, "He will not continue his quotation; in truth, he scornfully considers it superfluous to talk of counterpoint to us poor Italians." Your Christian name is Johann?—you are Herr Johannes. Look at her well. I shall not expose you longer than ten minutes to their observation. Frown meditative; the elbow propped and two fingers in the left cheek; and walk into the room with a stoop: touch a note of the piano, leaning your ear to it as in detection of five-fifteenths of a shade of discord. Frown in trouble as of a tooth. So, when you smile, it is immense praise to them, and easy for you.'

The names of the Signor Antonio-Pericles and Herr Johannes were taken up to the maestro.

Tormented with curiosity, Luigi saw them enter the house. The face and the martial or sanguinary reputation of Captain Weisspriess were not unknown to him. 'What has he to do with this affair?' thought Luigi, and sauntered down to the captain's servant, who accepted a cigar from him, but was rendered incorruptible by ignorance of his language. He observed that the horses were fresh, and were furnished with saddle-bags as for an expedition. What expedition? To serve as escort to the carriage?—a nonsensical idea. But the discovery that an idea is nonsensical is not a satisfactory solution of a difficulty. Luigi squatted on his haunches beside the doorstep, a little under one of the lower windows of Rocco Ricci's house. Earlier than he expected, the captain and Signor Antonio came out; and as soon as the door had closed behind them, the captain exclaimed, 'I give you my hand on it, my brave Pericles. You have done me many services, but this is finest of all. She's superb. She's a nice little wild woman to tame. I shall go to the Sonnenberg immediately. I have only to tell General Pierson that his nephew is to be prevented from playing the fool, and I get leave at once, if there's no active work.'

'His nephew, Lieutenant Pierson, or Pole—hein?' interposed the Greek.

'That's the man. He's on the Marshal's staff. He's engaged to the Countess Lena von Lenkenstein. She has fire enough, my Pericles.'

'The Countess Anna, you say?' The Greek stretched forward his ear, and was never so near getting it vigorously cuffed.

'Deafness is an unpardonable offence, my dear Pericles.'

Antonio-Pericles sniffed, and assented, 'It is the stupidity of the ear.'

'I said, the Countess Lena.'

'Von Lenkenstein; but I choose to be further deaf.'

'To the devil, sir. Do you pretend to be angry?' cried Weisspriess.

'The devil, sir, with your recommendation, is too black for me to visit him,' Antonio-Pericles rejoined.

'By heaven, Pericles, for less than what you allow yourself to say, I've sent men to him howling!'

They faced one another, pulling at their moustachios. Weisspriess laughed.

'You're not a fighting man, Pericles.'

The Greek nodded affably. 'One is in my way, I have him put out of my way. It is easiest.'

'Ah! easiest, is it?' Captain Weisspriess 'frowned meditative' over this remarkable statement of a system. 'Well, it certainly saves trouble. Besides, my good Pericles, none but an ass would quarrel with you. I was observing that General Pierson wants his nephew to marry the Countess Lena immediately; and if, as you tell me, this girl Belloni, who is called la Vittoria—the precious little woman!—has such power over him, it's quite as well, from the General's point of view, that she should be out of the way at Sonnenberg. I have my footing at the Duchess of Graath's. I believe she hopes that I shall some day challenge and kill her husband; and as I am supposed to have saved Major de Pyrmont's life, I am also an object of present gratitude. Do you imagine that your little brown-eyed Belloni scented one of her enemies in me?'

'I know nothing of imagination,' the Signor Antonio observed frigidly.

'Till we meet!' Captain Weisspriess kissed his fingers, half as up toward the windows, and half to the Greek. 'Save me from having to teach love to your Irma!'

He ran to join his servant.

Luigi had heard much of the conversation, as well as the last sentence.

'It shall be to la Irma if it is to anybody,' Luigi muttered.

'Let Weisspriess—he will not awake love in her—let him kindle hate, it will do,' said the Signor Antonio. 'She has seen him, and if he meets her on the route to Meran, she will think it her fascination.'

Looking at his watch and at the lighted windows, he repeated his special injunctions to Luigi. 'It is near the time. I go to sleep. I am getting old: I grow nervous. Ten-twenty in addition, you shall have, if all is done right. Your weekly pay runs on. Twenty — you shall have thirty! Thirty napoleons additional!'

Ten fingers were flashed thrice.

Luigi gave a jump. 'Padrone, they are mine.'

'Animal, that shake your belly-bag and brain-box, stand!' cried the Greek, who desired to see Luigi standing firm that he might inspire himself with confidence in his integrity. When Luigi's posture had satisfied him, he turned and went off at great strides.

'He does pay,' Luigi reflected, seeing that immense virtue in his patron. 'Yes, he pays; but what is he about? It is this question for me — "Do I serve my hand? or, Do I serve my heart?" My hand takes the money, and it is not German money. My heart gives the affection, and the signorina has my heart. She reached me that cigarette on the Motterone like the Madonna: it is never to be forgotten! I serve my heart! Now, Beppo, you may come; come quick for her. I see the carriage, and there are three stout fellows in it who could trip and muzzle you at a signal from me before you could count the letters of your father's baptismal name. Oh! but if the signorina disobeys me and comes out last! — the Signor Antonio will ask the maestro, who will say, "Yes, la Vittoria was here with me last of the two"; and I lose my ten, my twenty, my thirty napoleons.'

Luigi's chest expanded largely with a melancholy draught of air.

The carriage meantime had become visible at the head of the street, where it remained within hearing of a whistle. One of the Milanese hired vehicles drove up to the maestro's door shortly after, and Luigi cursed it. His worst fears for the future of the thirty napoleons were confirmed; the door opened and the Maestro Rocco Ricci, bareheaded and in his black silk dressing-gown, led out Irma di Karski, by some called rival to la Vittoria; a tall Slavic damsel, whose laughter was not soft and smooth, whose cheeks were bright, and whose eyes were deep in the head and dull. But she had vivacity both of lips and shoulders. The shoulders were bony; the lips were sharp and red, like winter-berries in the morning-time. Freshness was not absent from her aspect. The critical objection was that it seemed a plastered freshness and not true bloom; or rather it was a savage and a hard, not a sweet freshness. Hence perhaps the name which distinguished her la Lazzeruola (crab apple). It was a freshness that did not invite the bite; sour to Italian taste.

She was apparently in vast delight. 'There will be a perfect inundation to-morrow night from Prague and Vienna to see me even in so miserable a part as Michiella,' she said. 'Here I am supposed to be a beginner; I am no debutante there.'

'I can believe it, I can believe it,' responded Rocco, bowing for her speedy departure.

'You are not satisfied with my singing of Michiella's score! Now, tell me, kind, good, harsh old master! you think that Miss Vittoria would sing it better. So do I. And I can sing another part better. You do not know my capacities.'

'I am sure there is nothing you would not attempt,' said Rocco, bowing resignedly.

'There never was question of my courage.'

'Yes, but courage, courage! away with your courage!' Rocco was spurred by his personal grievances against her in a manner to make him forget his desire to be rid of her. 'Your courage sets you flying at once at every fioritura and bravura passage, to subdue, not to learn: not to accomplish, but to conquer it. And the ability, let me say, is not in proportion to the courage, which is probably too great to be easily equalled; but you have the opportunity to make your part celebrated to-morrow night, if, as you tell me, the house is to be packed with Viennese, and, signorina, you let your hair down.'

The hair of Irma di Karski was of singular beauty, and so dear to her that the allusion to the triumphant feature of her person passed off Rocco's irony in sugar.

'Addio! I shall astonish you before many hours have gone by,' she said; and this time they bowed together, and the maestro tripped back hurriedly, and shut his door.

Luigi's astonishment eclipsed his chagrin when he beheld the lady step from her place, bidding the driver move away as if he carried a freight, and indicating a position for him at the end of the street, with an imperative sway and deflection of her hand. Luigi heard the clear thin sound of a key dropped to her from one of the upper windows. She was quick to seize it; the door opened stealthily to her, and she passed out of sight without casting a look behind. 'That's a woman going to discover a secret, if she can,' remarked the observer; meaning that he considered the sex bad Generals, save when they have occasion to preserve themselves secret; then they look behind them carefully enough. The situation was one of stringent torment to a professional and natural spy. Luigi lost count of minutes in his irritation at the mystery, which he took as a personal offence. Some suspicion or wariness existed in the lighted room, for the maestro threw up a window, and inspected the street to right and left. Apparently satisfied he withdrew his head, and the window was closed.

In a little while Vittoria's voice rose audible out of the stillness, though she restrained its volume.

Its effect upon Luigi was to make him protest to her, whimpering with pathos as if she heard and must be melted: 'Signorina! signorina, most dear! for charity's sake! I am one of you; I am a patriot. Every man to his trade, but my heart is all with you.' And so on, louder by fits, in a running murmur, like one having his conscience ransacked, from which he was diverted by a side-thought of Irma di Karski, la Lazzeruola, listening, taking poison in at her ears; for Luigi had no hesitation in ascribing her behaviour to jealousy. 'Does not that note drive through your bosom, excellent lady? I can fancy the tremble going all down your legs. You are poisoned with honey. How you hate it! If you only had a dagger!'

Vittoria sang but for a short space. Simultaneously with the cessation of her song Ammiani reached the door, but had scarcely taken his stand there when, catching sight of Luigi, he crossed the street, and recognizing him, questioned him sternly as to his business opposite the maestro's house. Luigi pointed to a female figure emerging. 'See! take her home,' he said. Ammiani released him and crossed back hurriedly, when, smiting his forehead, Luigi cried in despair, 'Thirty napoleons and my professional reputation lost!' He blew a whistle; the carriage dashed down from the head of the street. While Ammiani was following the swiftly-stepping figure in wonderment (knowing it could not be Vittoria, yet supposing it must be, without any clear aim of his wits), the carriage drew up a little in advance of her; three men — men of bulk and sinew jumped from it; one threw himself upon Ammiani, the others grasped the affrighted lady, tightening a veil over her face, and the carriage- door shut sharp upon her. Ammiani's assailant then fell away: Luigi flung himself on the box and shouted, 'The signorina is behind you!' And Ammiani beheld Vittoria standing in alarm, too joyful to know that it was she. In the spasm of joy he kissed her hands. Before they could intercommunicate intelligibly the carriage was out of their sight, going at a gallop along the eastern strada of the circumvallation of the city.

CHAPTER XV
AMMIANI THROUGH THE MIDNIGHT

Ammiani hurried Vittoria out of the street to make safety sure. 'Home,' she said, ashamed of her excitement, and not daring to speak more words, lest the heart in her throat should betray itself. He saw what the fright had done for her. Perhaps also he guessed that she was trying to conceal her fancied cowardice from him. 'I have kissed her hands,' he thought, and the memory of it was a song of tenderness in his blood by the way.

Vittoria's dwelling-place was near the Duomo, in a narrow thoroughfare leading from the Duomo to the Piazza of La Scala, where a confectioner of local fame conferred upon the happier members of the population most piquant bocconi and tartlets, and offered by placard to give an emotion to the nobility, the literati, and the epicures of Milan, and to all foreigners, if the aforesaid would adventure upon a trial of his art. Meanwhile he let lodgings. It was in the house of this famous confectioner Zotti that Vittoria and her mother had lived after leaving England for Italy. As Vittoria came under the fretted shadow of the cathedral, she perceived her mother standing with Zotti at the house- door, though the night was far advanced. She laughed, and walked less hurriedly. Ammiani now asked her if she had been alarmed. 'Not alarmed,' she said, 'but a little more nervous than I thought I should be.'

He was spared from putting any further question by her telling him that Luigi, the Motterone spy, had in all probability done her a service in turning one or other f the machinations of the Signor Antonio. 'My madman,' she called this latter. 'He has got his Irma instead of me. We shall have to supply her place tomorrow; she is travelling rapidly, and on my behalf! I think, Signor Carlo, you would do well by going to the maestro when you leave me, and telling him that Irma has been caught into the skies. Say, "Jealous that earth should possess such overpowering loveliness," or "Attracted in spite of themselves by that combination of genius and beauty which is found united nowhere but in Irma, the spirits of heaven determined to rob earth of her Lazzeruola." Only tell it to him seriously, for my dear Rocco will have to work with one of the singers all day, and I ought to be at hand by them to help her, if I dared stir out. What do you think?'

Ammiani pronounced his opinion that it would be perilous for her to go abroad.

'I shall in truth, I fear, have a difficulty in getting to La Scala unseen,' she said; 'except that we are cunning people in our house. We not only practise singing and invent wonderful confectionery, but we do conjuring tricks. We profess to be able to deceive anybody whom we please.'

'Do the dupes enlist in a regiment?' said Ammiani, with an intonation that professed his readiness to serve as a recruit. His humour striking with hers, they smiled together in the bright fashion of young people who can lose themselves in a ray of fancy at any season.

Vittoria heard her mother's wailful voice. 'Twenty gnats in one,' she said.

Ammiani whispered quickly to know whether she had decided for the morrow.
She nodded, and ran up to her mother, who cried:

'At this hour! And Beppo has been here after you, and he told me I wrote for him, in Italian, when not a word can I put to paper: I wouldn't! — and you are threatened by dreadful dangers, he declares. His behaviour was mad; they are all mad over in this country, I believe. I have put the last stitch to your dress. There is a letter or two upstairs for you. Always letters!'

'My dear good Zotti,' Vittoria turned to the artist in condiments, 'you must insist upon my mother going to bed at her proper time when I am out.'

'Signorina,' rejoined Zotti, a fat little round-headed man, with vivacious starting brown eyes, 'I have only to tell her to do a thing — I pull a dog by the collar; be it said with reverence.'

'However, I am very glad to see you both such good friends.'

'Yes, signorina, we are good friends till we quarrel again. I regret to observe to you that the respectable lady is incurably suspicious. Of me —Zotti! Mother of heaven!'

'It is you that are suspicious of me, sir,' retorted madame. 'Of me, of all persons! It's "tell me this, tell me that," all day with you; and because I can't answer, you are angry.'

'Behold! the signora speaks English; we have quarrelled again,' said Zotti.

'My mother thinks him a perfect web of plots,' Vittoria explained the case between them, laughing, to Ammiani; 'and Zotti is persuaded that she is an inveterate schemer. They are both entirely innocent, only they are both excessively timid. Out of that it grows.'

The pair dramatized her outline on the instant:

'"Did I not see him speak to an English lady, and he will not tell me a word about it, though she's my own countrywoman?"'

'"Is it not true that she received two letters this afternoon, and still does she pretend to be ignorant of what is going on?"'

'Happily,' said Vittoria, 'my mother is not a widow, or these quarrels might some day end in a fearful reconciliation.'

'My child,' her mother whimpered, 'you know what these autumn nights are in this country; as sure as you live, Emilia, you will catch cold, and then you're like a shop with shutters up for the dead.'

At the same time Zotti whispered: 'Signorina, I have kept the minestra hot for your supper; come in, come in. And, little things, little dainty bits!—do you live in Zotti's house for nothing? Sweetest delicacies that make the tongue run a stream!—just notions of a taste—the palate smacks and forgets; the soul seizes and remembers!'

'Oh, such seductions!' Vittoria exclaimed.

'It is,' Zotti pursued his idea, with fingers picturesquely twirling in a spider-like distension; 'it is like the damned, and they have but a crumb of a chance of Paradise, and down swoops St. Peter and has them in the gates fast! You are worthy of all that a man can do for you, signorina. Let him study, let him work, let him invent,—you are worthy of all.'

'I hope I am not too hungry to discriminate! Zotti I see Monte Rosa.'

'Signorina, you are pleased to say so when you are famishing. It is because—' the enthusiastic confectioner looked deep and oblique, as one who combined a remarkable subtlety of insight with profound reflection; 'it is because the lighter you get the higher you mount; up like an eagle of the peaks! But we'll give that hungry fellow a fall. A dish of hot minestra shoots him dead. Then, a tart of pistachios and chocolate and cream—and my head to him who shall reveal to me the flavouring!'

'When I wake in the morning, I shall have lived a month or two in Arabia,

Zotti. Tell me no more; I will come in,' said Vittoria.

'Then, signorina, a little crisp filbert—biscuit—a composition! You crack it, and a surprise! And then, and then my dish; Zotti's dish, that is not yet christened. Signorina, let Italy rise first; the great inventor of the dish winked and nodded temperately. 'Let her rise. A battle or a treaty will do. I have two or three original conceptions, compositions, that only wait for some brilliant feat of arms, or a diplomatic triumph, and I send them forth baptized.'

Vittoria threw large eyes upon Ammiani, and set the underlids humorously quivering. She kissed her fingers: 'Addio; a rivederla.' He bowed formally: he was startled to find the golden thread of their companionship cut with such cruel abruptness. But it was cut; the door had closed on her. The moment it had closed she passed into his imagination. By what charm had she allayed the fever of his anxiety? Her naturalness had perforce given him assurance that peace must surround one in whom it shone so steadily, and smiling at the thought of Zotti's repast and her twinkle of subdued humour, he walked away comforted; which, for a lover in the season of peril means exalted, as in a sudden conflagration of the dry stock of his intelligence. 'She must have some great faith in her heart,' he thought, no longer attributing his exclusion from it to a lover's rivalry, which will show that more than imagination was on fire within him. For when the soul of a youth can be heated above common heat, the vices of passion shrivel up and aid the purer flame. It was well for Ammiani that he did perceive (dimly though it was perceived) the force of idealistic inspiration by which Vittoria was supported. He saw it at this one moment, and it struck a light to light him in many subsequent perplexities; it was something he had never seen before. He had read Tuscan poetry to her in old Agostino's rooms; he had spoken of secret preparations for the revolt; he had declaimed upon Italy, — the poetry was good though the declamation may have been bad, — but she had always been singularly irresponsive, with a practical turn for ciphers. A quick reckoning, a sharp display of figures in Italy's cause, kindled her cheeks and took her breath. Ammiani now understood that there lay an unspoken depth in her, distinct from her visible nature.

He had first an interview with Rocco Ricci, whom he prepared to replace
Irma.

His way was then to the office of his Journal, where he expected to be greeted by two members of the Polizia, who would desire him to march before the central bureau, and exhibit proofs of articles and the items of news for inspection, for correction haply, and possibly for approval. There is a partial delight in the contemplated submission to an act of servitude for the last time. Ammiani stepped in with combative gaiety, but his stiff glance encountered no enemy. This astonished him. He turned back into the street and meditated. The Pope's Mouth might, he thought, hold the key to the riddle. It is not always most comfortable for a conspirator to find himself unsuspected: he reads the blank significantly. It looked ill that the authorities should allow anything whatsoever to be printed on such a morrow: especially ill, if they were on the alert. The neighbourhood by the Pope's Mouth was desolate under dark starlight. Ammiani got his fingers into the opening behind the rubbish of brick, and tore them on six teeth of a saw that had been fixed therein. Those teeth were as voluble to him as loud tongues. The Mouth was empty of any shred of paper. They meant that the enemy was ready to bite, and that the conspiracy had ceased to be active. He perceived that a stripped ivy-twig, with the leaves scattered around it, stretched at his feet. That was another and corroborative sign, clearer to him than printed capitals. The reading of it declared that the Revolt had collapsed. He wound and unwound his handkerchief about his fingers mechanically: great curses were in his throat. 'I would start for South America at dawn, but for her!' he said. The country of Bolivar still had its attractions for Italian youth. For a certain space Ammiani's soul was black with passion. He was the son of that fiery Paolo Ammiani who had cast his glove at Eugene's feet, and bade the viceroy deliver it to his French master. (The General was preparing to break his sword on his knee when Eugene rushed up to him and kissed him.) Carlo was of this blood. Englishmen will hardly forgive him for having tears in his eyes, but Italians follow the Greek classical prescription for the emotions, while we take example by the Roman. There is no sneer due from us. He sobbed. It seemed that a country was lost.

Ammiani had moved away slowly: he was accidentally the witness of a curious scene. There came into the irregular triangle, and walking up to where the fruitstalls stood by day, a woman and a man. The man was an Austrian soldier. It was an Italian woman by his side. The sight of the couple was just then like an incestuous horror to Ammiani. She led the soldier straight up to the Mouth, directing his hand to it, and, what was far more wonderful, directing it so that he drew forth a packet of papers from where Ammiani had found none. Ammiani could see the light of them in his hand. The Austrian snatched an embrace and ran. Ammiani was moving over to her to seize and denounce the traitress, when he beheld another figure like an apparition by her side; but this one was not a whitecoat. Had it risen from the earth? It was earthy, for a cloud of dust was about it, and the woman gave a stifled scream. 'Barto! Barto!' she cried, pressing upon her eyelids. A strong husky laugh came from him. He tapped her shoulder heartily, and his 'Ha! ha!' rang in the night air.

'You never trust me,' she whimpered from shaken nerves.

He called her, 'Brave little woman! rare girl!'

'But you never trust me!'

'Do I not lay traps to praise you?'

'You make a woman try to deceive you.' If she could! If only she could!'

Ammiani was up with them.

'You are Barto Rizzo,' he spoke, half leaning over the man in his impetuosity.

Barto stole a defensive rearward step. The thin light of dawn had in a moment divided the extreme starry darkness, and Ammiani, who knew his face, had not to ask a second time. It was scored by a recent sword-cut. He glanced at the woman: saw that she was handsome.

It was enough; he knew she must be Barto's wife, and, if not more cunning than Barto, his accomplice, his instrument, his slave.

'Five minutes ago I would have sworn you were a traitress he said to her.

She was expressionless, as if she had heard nothing; which fact, considering that she was very handsome, seemed remarkable to the young man. Youth will not believe that stupidity and beauty can go together.

'She is the favourite pupil of Bartolommeo Rizzo, Signor Carlo Ammiani,' quoth Barto, having quite regained his composure. 'She is my pretty puppet-patriot. I am not in the habit of exhibiting her; but since you see her, there she is.'

Barto had fallen into the Southern habit of assuming ease in quasi-rhetorical sentences, but with wary eyes over them. The peculiar, contracting, owl-like twinkle defied Ammiani's efforts to penetrate his look; so he took counsel of his anger, and spoke bluntly.

'She does your work?'

'Much of it, Signor Carlo: as the bullet does the work of the rifle.'

'Beast! was it your wife who pinned the butterfly to the Signorina Vittoria's dress?'

'Signor Carlo Ammiani, you are the son of Paolo, the General: you call me beast? I have dandled you in my arms, my little lad, while the bands played "There's yet a heart in Italy!" Do you remember it?' Barto sang out half-a-dozen bars. 'You call me beast? I'm the one man in Milan who can sing you that.'

'Beast or man, devil or whatever you are!' cried Ammiani, feeling nevertheless oddly unnerved, 'you have committed a shameful offence: you, or the woman, your wife, who serves you, as I see. You have thwarted the best of plots; you have dared to act in defiance of your Chief —'

'Eyes to him!' Barto interposed, touching over his eyeballs.

'And you have thrown your accursed stupid suspicions on the Signorina Vittoria. You are a mad fool. If I had the power, I would order you to be shot at five this morning; and that 's the last rising of the light you should behold. Why did you do it? Don't turn your hellish eyes in upon one another, but answer at once! Why did you do it?'

'The Signorina Vittoria,' returned Barto—his articulation came forth serpent-like—'she is not a spy, you think. She has been in England: I have been in England. She writes; I can read. She is a thing of whims. Shall she hold the goblet of Italy in her hand till it overflows? She writes love-letters to an English whitecoat. I have read them. Who bids her write? Her whim! She warns her friends not to enter Milan. She— whose puppet is she? Not yours; not mine. She is the puppet of an English Austrian!'

Barto drew back, for Ammiani was advancing.

'What is it you mean?' he cried.

'I mean,' said Ammiani, still moving on him, 'I mean to drag you first before Count Medole, and next before the signorina; and you shall abjure your slander in her presence. After that I shall deal with you. Mark me! I have you: I am swifter on foot, and I am stronger. Come quietly.'

Barto smiled in grim contempt.

'Keep your foot fast on that stone, you're a prisoner,' he replied, and seeing Ammiani coming, 'Net him, my sling-stone! my serpent!' he signalled to his wife, who threw herself right round Ammiani in a tortuous twist hard as wire-rope. Stung with irritation, and a sense of disgrace and ridicule and pitifulness in one, Ammiani, after a struggle, ceased the attempt to disentwine her arms, and dragged her clinging to him. He was much struck by hearing her count deliberately, in her desperation, numbers from somewhere about twenty to one hundred. One hundred was evidently the number she had to complete, for when she had reached it she threw her arms apart. Barto was out of sight. Ammiani waved her on to follow in his steps: he was sick of her presence, and had the sensations of a shame-faced boy whom a girl has kissed. She went without uttering a word.

The dawn had now traversed the length of the streets, and thrown open the wide spaces of the city. Ammiani found himself singing, 'There's yet a heart in Italy!' but it was hardly the song of his own heart. He slept that night on a chair in the private room of his office, preferring not to go to his mother's house. 'There 's yet a heart in Italy!' was on his lips when he awoke with scattered sensations, all of which collected in revulsion against the song. 'There's a very poor heart in Italy!' he said, while getting his person into decent order;

'it's like the bell in the lunatic's tower between Venice and the Lido: it beats now and then for meals: hangs like a carrion-lump in the vulture's beak meanwhile!'

These and some other similar sentiments, and a heat about the brows whenever he set them frowning over what Barto had communicated concerning an English Austrian, assured Ammiani that he had no proper command of himself: or was, as the doctors would have told him, bilious. It seemed to him that he must have dreamed of meeting the dark and subtle Barto Rizzo overnight; on realizing that fact he could not realize how the man had escaped him, except that when he thought over it, he breathed deep and shook his shoulders. The mind will, as you may know, sometimes refuse to work when the sensations are shameful and astonished. He despatched a messenger with a 'good morrow' to his mother, and then went to a fencing-saloon that was fitted up in the house of Count Medole, where, among two or three, there was the ordinary shrugging talk of the collapse of the projected outbreak, bitter to hear. Luciano Romara came in, and Ammiani challenged him to small-sword and broadsword. Both being ireful to boiling point, and mad to strike at something, they attacked one another furiously, though they were dear friends, and the helmet- wires and the padding rattled and smoked to the thumps. For half an hour they held on to it, when, their blood being up, they flashed upon the men present, including the count, crying shame to them for letting a woman alone be faithful to her task that night. The blood forsook Count Medole's cheeks, leaving its dead hue, as when blotting-paper is laid on running-ink. He deliberately took a pair of foils, and offering the handle of one to Ammiani, broke the button off the end of his own, and stood to face an adversary. Ammiani followed the example: a streak of crimson was on his shirt-sleeve, and his eyes had got their hard black look, as of the flint-stone, before Romara in amazement discovered the couple to be at it in all purity of intention, on the sharp edge of the abyss. He knocked up their weapons and stood between them, puffing his cigarette leisurely.

'I fine you both,' he said.

He touched Ammiani's sword-arm, nodded with satisfaction to find that there was no hurt, and cried, 'You have an Austrian out on the ground by this time tomorrow morning. So, according to the decree!'

'Captain Weisspriess is in the city,' was remarked.

'There are a dozen on the list,' said little Pietro Cardi, drawing out a paper.

'If you are to be doing nothing else to-morrow morning,' added Leone Rufo, 'we may as well march out the whole dozen.'

These two were boys under twenty.

'Shall it be the first hit for Captain Weisspriess?' Count Medole said this while handing a fresh and fairly-buttoned foil to Ammiani.

Romara laughed: 'You will require to fence the round of Milan city, my dear count, to win a claim to Captain Weisspriess. In the first place, I yield him to no man who does not show himself a better man than I. It's the point upon which I don't pay compliments.'

Count Medole bowed.

'But, if you want occupation,' added Luciano, closing his speech with a merely interrogative tone.

'I scarcely want that, as those who know me will tell you,' said Medole, so humbly, that those who knew him felt that he had risen to his high seat of intellectual contempt. He could indulge himself, having shown his courage.

'Certainly not; if you are devising means of subsistence for the widows and orphans of the men who will straggle out to be slaughtered to-night,' said Luciano; 'you have occupation in that case.'

'I will do my best to provide for them,' — the count persisted in his air of humility, 'though it is a question with some whether idiots should live.' He paused effectively, and sucked in a soft smile of self-approbation at the stroke. Then he pursued: 'We meet the day after to-morrow. The Pope's Mouth is closed. We meet here at nine in the morning. The next day at eleven at Farugino's, the barber's, in Monza. The day following at Camerlata, at eleven likewise. Those who attend will be made aware of the dispositions for the week, and the day we shall name for the rising. It is known to you all, that without affixing a stigma on our new prima-donna, we exclude her from any share in this business. All the Heads have been warned that we yield this night to the Austrians. Gentlemen, I cannot be more explicit. I wish that I could please you better.'

'Oh, by all means,' said Pietro Cardi: 'but patience is the pestilence; I shall roam in quest of adventure. Another quiet week is a tremendous trial.'

He crossed foils with Leone Rufo, but finding no stop to the drawn 'swish' of the steel, he examined the end of his weapon with a lengthening visage, for it was buttonless. Ammiani burst into laughter at the spontaneous boyishness in the faces of the pair of ambitious lads. They both offered him one of the rapiers upon equal terms. Count Medole's example of intemperate vanity was spoiling them.

'You know my opinion,' Ammiani said to the count. 'I told you last night, and I tell you again to-day, that Barto Rizzo is guilty of gross misconduct, and that you must plead the same to a sort of excuseable treason. Count Medole, you cannot wind and unwind a conspiracy like a watch. Who is the head of this one? It is the man Barto Rizzo. He took proceedings before he got you to sanction them. You may be the vessel, but he commands, or at least, he steers it.'

The count waited undemonstratively until Ammiani had come to an end. 'You speak, my good Ammiani, with an energy that does you credit,' he said, 'considering that it is not in your own interest, but another person's. Remember, I can bear to have such a word as treason ascribed to my acts.'

Fresh visitors, more or less mixed, in the conspiracy, and generally willing to leave the management of it to Count Medole, now entered the saloon. These were Count Rasati, Angelo Dovili, a Piedmontese General, a Tuscan duke, and one or two aristocratic notabilities and historic nobodies. They were hostile to the Chief whom Luciano and Carlo revered and obeyed. The former lit a cigarette, and saying to his friend, 'Do you breakfast with your mother? I will come too,' slipped his hand on Ammiani's arm; they walked out indolently together, with the smallest shade of an appearance of tolerating scorn for those whom they left behind.

'Medole has money and rank and influence, and a kind of I-don't-know-what womanishness, that makes him push like a needle for the lead, and he will have the lead and when he has got the lead, there 's the last chapter of him,' said Luciano. 'His point of ambition is the perch of the weather- cock. Why did he set upon you, my Carlo? I saw the big V running up your forehead when you faced him. If you had finished him no great harm would have been done.'

'I saw him for a short time last night, and spoke to him in my father's style,' said Carlo. 'The reason was, that he defended Barto Rizzo for putting the ring about the Signorina Vittoria's name, and causing the black butterfly to be pinned to her dress.'

Luciano's brows stood up.

'If she sings to-night, depend upon it there will be a disturbance,' he said. 'There may be a rising in spite of Medole and such poor sparks, who're afraid to drop on powder, and twirl and dance till the wind blows them out. And mind, the chance rising is commonly the luckiest. If I get a command I march to the Alps. We must have the passes of the Tyrol. It seems to me that whoever holds the Alps must ride the Lombard mare. You spring booted and spurred into the saddle from the Alps.'

Carlo was hurt by his friend's indifference to the base injury done to Vittoria.

'I have told Medole that she will sing to-night in spite of him,' he was saying, with the intention of bringing round some reproach upon Luciano for his want of noble sympathy, when the crash of an Austrian regimental band was heard coming up the Corso. It stirred him to love his friend with all his warmth. 'At any rate, for my sake, Luciano, you will respect and uphold her.'

'Yes, while she's true,' said Luciano, unsatisfactorily. The regiment, in review uniform, followed by two pieces of artillery, passed by. Then came a squadron of hussars and one of Uhlans, and another foot regiment, more artillery, fresh cavalry.

'Carlo, if three generations of us pour out our blood to fertilize Italian ground, it's not too much to pay to chase those drilled curs.' Luciano spoke in vehement undertone.

'We 'll breakfast and have a look at them in the Piazza d'Armi, and show that we Milanese are impressed with a proper idea of their power,' said Carlo, brightening as he felt the correction of his morbid lover's anger in Luciano's reaching view of their duties as Italian citizens. The heat and whirl of the hour struck his head, for to-morrow they might be wrestling with that living engine which had marched past, and surely all the hate he could muster should be turned upon the outer enemy. He gained his mother's residence with clearer feelings.

CHAPTER XVI
COUNTESS AMMIANI

Countess Ammiani was a Venetian lady of a famous House, the name of which is as a trumpet sounding from the inner pages of the Republic. Her face was like a leaf torn from an antique volume; the hereditary features told the story of her days. The face was sallow and fireless; life had faded like a painted cloth upon the imperishable moulding. She had neither fire in her eyes nor colour on her skin. The thin close multitudinous wrinkles ran up accurately ruled from the chin to the forehead's centre, and touched faintly once or twice beyond, as you observe the ocean ripples run in threads confused to smoothness within a space of the grey horizon sky. But the chin was firm, the mouth and nose were firm, the forehead sat calmly above these shows of decay. It was a most noble face; a fortress face; strong and massive, and honourable in ruin, though stripped of every flower.

This lady in her girlhood had been the one lamb of the family dedicated to heaven. Paolo, the General, her lover, had wrenched her from that fate to share with him a life of turbulent sorrows till she should behold the blood upon his grave. She, like Laura Fiaveni, had bent her head above a slaughtered husband, but, unlike Laura, Marcellina Ammiani had not buried her heart with him. Her heart and all her energies had been his while he lived; from the visage of death it turned to her son. She had accepted the passion for Italy from Paolo; she shared it with Carlo. Italian girls of that period had as little passion of their own as flowers kept out of sunlight have hues. She had given her son to her country with that intensely apprehensive foresight of a mother's love which runs quick as Eastern light from the fervour of the devotion to the remote realization of the hour of the sacrifice, seeing both in one. Other forms of love, devotion in other bosoms, may be deluded, but hers will not be. She sees the sunset in the breast of the springing dawn. Often her son Carlo stood a ghost in her sight. With this haunting prophetic vision, it was only a mother, who was at the same time a supremely noble woman, that could feel all human to him notwithstanding. Her heart beat thick and fast when Carlo and Luciano entered the morning- room where she sat, and stopped to salute her in turn.

'Well?' she said without betraying anxiety or playing at carelessness.

Carlo answered, 'Let us eat and drink, for to-morrow we die. I think that's the language of peaceful men.'

'You are to be peaceful men to-morrow, my Carlo?'

'The thing is in Count Medole's hands,' said Luciano; 'and he is constitutionally of our Agostino's opinion that we are bound to wait till the Gods kick us into action; and, as Agostino says, Medole has raised himself upon our shoulders so as to be the more susceptible to their wishes when they blow a gale.'

He informed her of the momentary thwarting of the conspiracy, and won
Carlo's gratitude by not speaking of the suspicion which had fallen on
Vittoria.

'Medole,' he said, 'has the principal conduct of the business in Milan, as you know, countess. Our Chief cannot be everywhere at once; so Medole undertakes to decide for him here in old Milan. He decided yesterday afternoon to put off our holiday for what he calls a week. Checco, the idiot, in whom he confides, gave me the paper signifying the fact at four o'clock. There was no appeal; for we can get no place of general meeting under Medole's prudent management. He fears our being swallowed in a body if we all meet.'

The news sent her heart sinking in short throbs down to a delicious rest; but Countess Ammiani disdained to be servile to the pleasure, even as she had strengthened herself to endure the shocks of pain. It was a conquered heart that she and every Venetian and Lombard mother had to carry; one that played its tune according to its nature, shaping no action, sporting no mask. If you know what is meant by that phrase, a conquered heart, you will at least respect them whom you call weak women for having gone through the harshest schooling which this world can show example of. In such mothers Italy revived. The pangs and the martyrdom were theirs. Fathers could march to the field or to the grey glacis with their boys; there was no intoxication of hot blood to cheer those who sat at home watching the rise and fall of trembling scales which said life or death for their dearest. Their least shadowy hope could be but a shrouded contentment in prospect; a shrouded submission in feeling. What bloom of hope was there when Austria stood like an iron wall, and their own ones dashing against it were as little feeble waves that left a red mark and no more? But, duty to their country had become their religion; sacrifice they accepted as their portion; when the last stern evil befell them they clad themselves in a veil and walked upon an earth they had passed from for all purposes save service of hands. Italy revived in these mothers. Their torture was that of the re-animation of her frame from the death-trance.

Carlo and Luciano fell hungrily upon dishes of herb-flavoured cutlets, and Neapolitan maccaroni, green figs, green and red slices of melon, chocolate, and a dry red Florentine wine. The countess let them eat, and then gave her son a letter that been delivered at her door an hour back by the confectioner Zotti. It proved to be an enclosure of a letter addressed to Vittoria by the Chief. Genoa was its superscription. From that place it was forwarded by running relays of volunteer messengers. There were points of Italy which the Chief could reach four-and-twenty hours in advance of the Government with all its aids and machinery. Vittoria had simply put her initials at the foot of the letter. Carlo read it eagerly and cast it aside. It dealt in ideas and abstract phraseology; he could get nothing of it between his impatient teeth; he was reduced to a blank wonder at the reason for her sending it on to him. It said indeed — and so far it seemed to have a meaning for her:

'No backward step. We can bear to fall; we cannot afford to draw back.'

And again:

'Remember that these uprisings are the manifested pulsations of the heart of your country, so that none shall say she is a corpse, and knowing that she lives, none shall say that she deserves not freedom. It is the protest of her immortal being against her impious violator.'

Evidently the Chief had heard nothing of the counterstroke of Barto Rizzo, and of Count Medole's miserable weakness: but how, thought Carlo, how can a mind like Vittoria's find matter to suit her in such sentences? He asked himself the question, forgetting that a little time gone by, while he was aloof from the tumult and dreaming of it, this airy cloudy language and every symbolism, had been strong sustaining food, a vital atmosphere, to him. He did not for the moment (though by degrees he recovered his last night's conception of her) understand that among the noble order of women there is, when they plunge into strife, a craving for idealistic truths, which men are apt, under the heat and hurry of their energies, to put aside as stars that are meant merely for shining.

His mother perused the letter—holding it out at arm's length—and laid it by; Luciano likewise. Countess Ammiani was an aristocrat: the tone and style of the writing were distasteful to her. She allowed her son's judgement of the writer to stand for her own, feeling that she could surrender little prejudices in favour of one who appeared to hate the Austrians so mortally. On the other hand, she defended Count Medole. Her soul shrank at the thought of the revolution being yielded up to theorists and men calling themselves men of the people—a class of men to whom Paolo her soldier-husband's aversion had always been formidably pronounced. It was an old and a wearisome task for Carlo to explain to her that the times were changed and the necessities of the hour different since the day when his father conspired and fought for freedom. Yet he could not gainsay her when she urged that the nobles should be elected to lead, if they consented to lead; for if they did not lead, were they not excluded from the movement?

'I fancy you have defined their patriotism,' said Carlo.

'Nay, my son; but you are one of them.'

'Indeed, my dearest mother, that is not what they will tell you.'

'Because you have chosen to throw yourself into the opposite ranks.'

'You perceive that you divide our camp, madame my mother. For me there is no natural opposition of ranks. What are we? We are slaves: all are slaves. While I am a slave, shall I boast that I am of noble birth? "Proud of a coronet with gems of paste!" some one writes. Save me from that sort of pride! I am content to take my patent of nobility for good conduct in the revolution. Then I will be count, or marquis, or duke; I am not a Republican pure blood;—but not till then. And in the meantime—'

'Carlo is composing for his newspaper,' the countess said to Luciano.

'Those are the leaders who can lead,' the latter replied. 'Give the men who are born to it the first chance. Old Agostino is right—the people owe them their vantage ground. But when they have been tried and they have failed, decapitate them. Medole looks upon revolution as a description of conjuring trick. He shuffles cards and arranges them for a solemn performance, but he refuses to cut them if you look too serious or I look too eager; for that gives him a suspicion that you know what is going to turn up; and his object is above all things to produce a surprise.'

'You are both of you unjust to Count Medole,' said the countess. 'He imperils more than all of you.'

'Magnificent estates, it is true; but of head or of heart not quite so much as some of us,' said Luciano, stroking his thick black pendent moustache and chin-tuft. 'Ah, pardon me; yes! he does imperil a finer cock's comb.

'When he sinks, and his vanity is cut in two, Medole will bleed so as to flood his Lombard flats. It will be worse than death to him.'

Carlo said: 'Do you know what our Agostino says of Count Medole?'

'Oh, for ever Agostino with you young men!' the countess exclaimed. 'I believe he laughs at you.'

'To be sure he does: he laughs at all. But, what he says of Count Medole holds the truth of the thing, and may make you easier concerning the count's estates. He says that Medole is vaccine matter which the Austrians apply to this generation of Italians to spare us the terrible disease. They will or they won't deal gently with Medole, by-and-by; but for the present he will be handled tenderly. He is useful. I wish I could say that we thought so too. And now,' Carlo stooped to her and took her hand, 'shall we see you at La Scala to-night?'

The countess, with her hands lying in his, replied: 'I have received an intimation from the authorities that my box is wanted.'

'So you claim your right to occupy it!'

'That is my very humble protest for personal liberty.'

'Good: I shall be there, and shall much enjoy an introduction to the gentleman who disputes it with you. Besides, mother, if the Signorina Vittoria sings . . .'

Countess Ammiani's gaze fixed upon her son with a level steadiness. His voice threatened to be unequal. All the pleading force of his eyes was thrown into it, as he said: 'She will sing: and she gives the signal; that is certain. We may have to rescue her. If I can place her under your charge, I shall feel that she is safe, and is really protected.'

The countess looked at Luciano before she answered:

'Yes, Carlo, whatever I can do. But you know I have not a scrap of influence.'

'Let her lie on your bosom, my mother.'

'Is this to be another Violetta?'

'Her name is Vittoria,' said Carlo, colouring deeply. A certain Violetta had been his boy's passion.

Further distracting Austrian band-music was going by. This time it was a regiment of Italians in the white and blue uniform. Carlo and Luciano leaned over the balcony, smoking, and scanned the marching of their fellow-countrymen in the livery of servitude.

'They don't step badly,' said one; and the other, with a smile of melancholy derision, said, 'We are all brothers!'

Following the Italians came a regiment of Hungarian grenadiers, tall, swam-faced, and particularly light-limbed men, looking brilliant in the clean tight military array of Austria. Then a squadron of blue hussars, and Croat regiment; after which, in the midst of Czech dragoons and German Uhlans and blue Magyar light horsemen, with General officers and aides about him, the veteran Austrian Field-Marshal rode, his easy hand and erect figure and good-humoured smile belying both his age and his reputation among Italians. Artillery, and some bravely-clad horse of the Eastern frontier, possibly Serb, wound up the procession. It gleamed down the length of the Corso in a blinding sunlight; brass helmets and hussar feathers, white and violet surcoats, green plumes, maroon capes, bright steel scabbards, bayonet-points,—as gallant a show as some portentously-magnified summer field, flowing with the wind, might be; and over all the banner of Austria—the black double-headed eagle ramping on a yellow ground. This was the flower of iron meaning on such a field.

The two young men held their peace. Countess Ammiani had pushed her chair back into a dark corner of the room, and was sitting there when they looked back, like a sombre figure of black marble.

CHAPTER XVII
IN THE PIAZZA D'ARMI

Carlo and Luciano followed the regiments to the Piazza d'Armi, drawn after them by that irresistible attraction to youths who have as yet had no shroud of grief woven for them—desire to observe the aspect of a brilliant foe.

The Piazza d'Armi was the field of Mars of Milan, and an Austrian review of arms there used to be a tropical pageant. The place was too narrow for broad manoeuvres, or for much more than to furnish an inspection of all arms to the General, and a display (with its meaning) to the populace. An unusually large concourse of spectators lined the square, like a black border to a vast bed of flowers, nodding now this way, now that. Carlo and Luciano passed among the groups, presenting the perfectly smooth faces of young men of fashion, according to the universal aristocratic pattern handed down to querulous mortals from Olympus—the secret of which is to show a triumphant inaction of the heart and the brain, that are rendered positively subservient to elegance of limb. They knew the chances were in favour of their being arrested at any instant. None of the higher members of the Milanese aristocracy were visible; the people looked sullen. Carlo was attracted by the tall figure of the Signor Antonio-Pericles, whom he beheld in converse with the commandant of the citadel, out in the square, among chatting and laughing General officers. At Carlo's elbow there came a burst of English tongues; he heard Vittoria's English name spoken with animation. 'Admire those faces,' he said to Luciano, but the latter was interchanging quiet recognitions among various heads of the crowd; a language of the eyelids and the eyebrows. When he did look round he admired the fair island faces with an Italian's ardour: 'Their women are splendid!' and he no longer pushed upon Carlo's arm to make way ahead. In the English group were two sunny-haired girls and a blue-eyed lady with the famous English curls, full, and rounding richly. This lady talked of her brother, and pointed him out as he rode down the line in the Marshal's staff. The young officer indicated presently broke away and galloped up to her, bending over his horse's neck to join the conversation. Emilia Belloni's name was mentioned. He stared, and appeared to insist upon a contrary statement.

Carlo scrutinized his features. While doing so he was accosted, and beheld his former adversary of the Motter—one, with whom he had yesterday shaken hands in the Piazza of La Scala. The ceremony was cordially renewed. Luciano unlinked his arm from Carlo and left him.

'It appears that you are mistaken with reference to Mademoiselle Belloni,' said Captain Gambier. 'We hear on positive authority that she will not appear at La Scala to-night. It's a disappointment; though, from what you did me the honour to hint to me, I cannot allow myself to regret it.'

Carlo had a passionate inward prompting to trust this Englishman with the secret. It was a weakness that he checked. When one really takes to foreigners, there is a peculiar impulse (I speak of the people who are accessible to impulse) to make brothers of them. He bowed, and said, 'She does not appear?'

'She has in fact quitted Milan. Not willingly. I would have stopped the business if I had known anything of it; but she is better out of the way, and will be carefully looked after, where she is. By this time she is in the Tyrol.'

'And where?' asked Carlo, with friendly interest.

'At a schloss near Meran. Or she will be there in a very few hours. I feared—I may inform you that we were very good friends in England— I feared that when she once came to Italy she would get into political scrapes. I dare say you agree with me that women have nothing to do with politics. Observe: you see the lady who is speaking to the Austrian officer?—he is her brother. Like Mademoiselle Belloni he has adopted a fresh name; it's the name of his uncle, a General Pierson in the Austrian service. I knew him in England: he has been in our service. Mademoiselle Belloni lived with his sisters for some years two or three. As you may suppose, they are all anxious to see her.

Shall I introduce. you? They will be glad to know one of her Italian friends.'

Carlo hesitated; he longed to hear those ladies talk of Vittoria. 'Do they speak French?'

'Oh, dear, yes. That is, as we luckless English people speak it. Perhaps you will more easily pardon their seminary Italian. See there,' Captain Gambier pointed at some trotting squadrons; 'these Austrians have certainly a matchless cavalry. The artillery seems good. The infantry are fine men—very fine men. They have a "woodeny" movement; but that's in the nature of the case: tremendous discipline alone gives homogeneity to all those nationalities. Somehow they get beaten. I doubt whether anything will beat their cavalry.'

'They are useless in street-fighting,' said Carlo.

'Oh, street-fighting!' Captain Gambier vented a soldier's disgust at the notion. 'They're not in Paris. Will you step forward?'

Just then the tall Greek approached the party of English. The introduction was delayed.

He was addressed by the fair lady, in the island tongue, as 'Mr. Pericles.' She thanked him for his extreme condescension in deigning to notice them. But whatever his condescension had been, it did not extend to an admitted acquaintance with the poor speech of the land of fogs. An exhibition of aching deafness was presented to her so resolutely, that at last she faltered, 'What! have you forgotten English, Mr. Pericles? You spoke it the other day.'

'It is ze language of necessity—of commerce,' he replied.

'But, surely, Mr. Pericles, you dare not presume to tell me you choose to be ignorant of it whenever you please?'

'I do not take grits into ze teeth, madame; no more.' 'But you speak it perfectly.'

'Perfect it may be, for ze transactions of commerce. I wish to keep my teez.'

'Alas!' said the lady, compelled, 'I must endeavour to swim in French.'

'At your service, madame,' quoth the Greek, with an immediate doubling of the length of his body.

Carlo heard little more than he knew; but the confirmation of what we know will sometimes instigate us like fresh intelligence, and the lover's heart was quick to apprehend far more than he knew in one direction. He divined instantaneously that the English-Austrian spoken of by Barto Rizzo was the officer sitting on horseback within half-a-dozen yards of him. The certainty of the thought cramped his muscles. For the rest, it became clear to him that the attempt of the millionaire connoisseur to carry off Vittoria had received the tacit sanction of the Austrian authorities; for reasons quite explicable, Mr. Pericles, as the English lady called him, distinctly hinted it, while affirming with vehement self-laudation that his scheme had succeeded for the vindication of Art.

'The opera you will hear zis night,' he said, 'will be hissed. You will hear a chorus of screech-owls to each song of that poor Irma, whom the Italian people call "crabapple." Well; she pleases German ears, and if they can support her, it is well. But la Vittoria—your Belloni—you will not hear; and why? She has been false to her Art, false! She has become a little devil in politics. It is a Guy Fawkes femelle! She has been guilty of the immense crime of ingratitude. She is dismissed to study, to penitence, and to the society of her old friends, if they will visit her.'

'Of course we will,' said the English lady; 'either before or after our visit to Venice—delicious Venice!'

'Which you have not seen—hein?' Mr. Pericles snarled; 'and have not smelt. There is no music in Venice! But you have nothing but street tinkle-tinkle! A place to live in! mon Dieu!'

The lady smiled. 'My husband insists upon trying the baths of Bormio, and then we are to go over a pass for him to try the grape-cure at Meran. If I can get him to promise me one whole year in Italy, our visit to Venice may be deferred. Our doctor, monsieur, indicates our route. If my brother can get leave of absence, we shall go to Bormio and to Meran with him. He is naturally astonished that Emilia refused to see him; and she refused to see us too! She wrote a letter, dated from the Conservatorio to him, he had it in his saddlebag, and was robbed of it and other precious documents, when the wretched, odious people set upon him in Verona-poor boy! She said in the letter that she would see him in a few days after the fifteenth, which is to-day!

'Ah! a few days after the fifteenth, which is to-day,' Mr. Pericles repeated. 'I saw you but the day before yesterday, madame, or I could have brought you together.

She is now away-off—out of sight—the perfule! Ah false that she is; speak not of her. You remember her in England. There it was trouble, trouble; but here, we are a pot on a fire with her; speak not of her. She has used me ill, madame. I am sick.'

His violent gesticulation drooped. In a temporary abandonment to chagrin, he wiped the moisture from his forehead, unwilling or heedless of the mild ironical mouthing of the ladies, and looked about; for Carlo had made a movement to retire,—he had heard enough for discomfort.

'Ah! my dear Ammiani, the youngest editor in Europe! how goes it with you?' the Greek called out with revived affability.

Captain Gambier perceived that it was time to present his Italian acquaintance to the ladies by name, as a friend of Mademoiselle Belloni.

'My most dear Ammiani,' Antonio-Pericles resumed; he barely attempted to conceal his acrid delight in casting a mysterious shadow of coming vexation over the youth; 'I am afraid you will not like the opera Camilla, or perhaps it is the Camilla you will not like. But, shoulder arms, march!' (a foot regiment in motion suggested the form of the recommendation) 'what is not for to-day may be for to-morrow. Let us wait. I think, my Ammiani, you are to have a lemon and not an orange. Never mind. Let us wait.'

Carlo got his forehead into a show of smoothness, and said, 'Suppose, my dear Signor Antonio, the prophet of dark things were to say to himself, "Let us wait?"'

'Hein-it is deep.' Antonio-Pericles affected to sound the sentence, eye upon earth, as a sparrow spies worm or crumb. 'Permit me,' he added rapidly; an idea had struck him from his malicious reserve stores,— 'Here is Lieutenant Pierson, of the staff of the Field-Marshal of Austria, unattached, an old friend of Mademoiselle Emilia Belloni,— permit me,—here is Count Ammiani, of the Lombardia Milanese journal, a new friend of the Signorina Vittoria Campa-Mademoiselle Belloni the Signorina Campa—it is the same person, messieurs; permit me to introduce you.'

Antonio-Pericles waved his arm between the two young men.

Their plain perplexity caused him to dash his fingers down each side of his moustachios in tugs of enjoyment.

For Lieutenant Pierson, who displayed a certain readiness to bow, had caught a sight of the repellent stare on Ammiani's face; a still and flat look, not aggressive, yet anything but inviting; like a shield.

Nevertheless, the lieutenant's head produced a stiff nod. Carlo's did not respond; but he lifted his hat and bowed humbly in retirement to the ladies.

Captain Gambier stepped aside with him.

'Inform Lieutenant Pierson, I beg you,' said Ammiani, 'that I am at his orders, if he should consider that I have insulted him.'

'By all means,' said Gambier; 'only, you know, it's impossible for me to guess what is the matter; and I don't think he knows.'

Luciano happened to be coming near. Carlo went up to him, and stood talking for half a minute. He then returned to Captain Gambier, and said, 'I put myself in the hands of a man of honour. You are aware that Italian gentlemen are not on terms with Austrian officers. If I am seen exchanging salutes with any one of them, I offend my countrymen; and they have enough to bear already.'

Perceiving that there was more in the background, Gambier simply bowed. He had heard of Italian gentlemen incurring the suspicion of their fellows by merely being seen in proximity to an Austrian officer.

As they were parting, Carlo said to him, with a very direct meaning in his eyes, 'Go to the opera tonight.'

'Yes, I suppose so,' the Englishman answered, and digested the look and the recommendation subsequently.

Lieutenant Pierson had ridden off. The war-machine was in motion from end to end: the field of flowers was a streaming flood; regiment by regiment, the crash of bands went by. Outwardly the Italians conducted themselves with the air of ordinary heedless citizens, in whose bosoms the music set no hell-broth boiling. Patrician and plebeian, they were chiefly boys; though here and there a middle-aged workman cast a look of intelligence upon Carlo and Luciano, when these two passed along the crowd. A gloom of hoarded hatred was visible in the mass of faces, ready to spring fierily.

Arms were in the city. With hatred to prompt the blow, with arms to strike, so much dishonour to avenge, we need not wonder that these youths beheld the bit of liberty in prospect magnified by their mighty obfuscating ardour, like a lantern in a fog. Reason did not act. They were in such a state when just to say 'Italia! Italia!' gave them nerve to match an athlete. So, the parading of Austria, the towering athlete, failed of its complete lesson of intimidation, and only ruffled the surface of insurgent hearts. It seemed, and it was, an insult to the trodden people, who read it as a lesson for cravens: their instinct commonly hits the bell. They felt that a secure supremacy would not have paraded itself: so they divined indistinctly that there was weakness somewhere in the councils of the enemy. When the show had vanished, their spirits hung pausing, like the hollow air emptied of big sound, and reacted. Austria had gained little more by her display than the conscientious satisfaction of the pedagogue who lifts the rod to advise intending juvenile culprits how richly it can be merited and how poor will be their future grounds of complaint.

But before Austria herself had been taught a lesson she conceived that she had but one man and his feeble instruments, and occasional frenzies, opposed to her, him whom we saw on the Motterone, which was ceasing to be true; though it was true that the whole popular movement flowed from that one man. She observed travelling sparks in the embers of Italy, and crushed them under her heel, without reflecting that a vital heat must be gathering where the spots of fire run with such a swiftness. It was her belief that if she could seize that one man, whom many of the younger nobles and all the people acknowledged as their Chief — for he stood then without a rival in his task — she would have the neck of conspiracy in her angry grasp. Had she caught him, the conspiracy for Italian freedom would not have crowed for many long seasons; the torch would have been ready, but not the magazine. He prepared it; it was he who preached to the Italians that opportunity is a mocking devil when we look for it to be revealed; or, in other words, wait for chance; as it is God's angel when it is created within us, the ripe fruit of virtue and devotion. He cried out to Italians to wait for no inspiration but their own; that they should never subdue their minds to follow any alien example; nor let a foreign city of fire be their beacon. Watching over his Italy; her wrist in his meditative clasp year by year; he stood like a mystic leech by the couch of a fair and hopeless frame, pledged to revive it by the inspired assurance, shared by none, that life had not forsaken it. A body given over to death and vultures-he stood by it in the desert. Is it a marvel to you that when the carrion-wings swooped low, and the claws fixed, and the beak plucked and savoured its morsel, he raised his arm, and urged the half-resuscitated frame to some vindicating show of existence? Arise! he said, even in what appeared most fatal hours of darkness. The slack limbs moved; the body rose and fell. The cost of the effort was the breaking out of innumerable wounds, old and new; the gain was the display of the miracle that Italy lived. She tasted her own blood, and herself knew that she lived.

Then she felt her chains. The time was coming for her to prove, by the virtues within her, that she was worthy to live, when others of her sons, subtle and adept, intricate as serpents, bold, unquestioning as well- bestridden steeds, should grapple and play deep for her in the game of worldly strife. Now—at this hour of which I speak—when Austrians marched like a merry flame down Milan streets, and Italians stood like the burnt-out cinders of the fire-grate, Italy's faint wrist was still in the clutch of her grave leech, who counted the beating of her pulse between long pauses, that would have made another think life to be heaving its last, not beginning.

The Piazza d'Armi was empty of its glittering show.

CHAPTER XVIII
THE NIGHT OF THE FIFTEENTH

We quit the Piazza d'Armi. Rumour had its home in Milan. On their way to the caffe La Scala, Luciano and Carlo (who held together, determined to be taken together if the arrest should come) heard it said that the Chief was in Milan. A man passed by and uttered it, going. They stopped a second man, who was known to them, and he confirmed the rumour. Glad as sunlight once more, they hurried to Count Medole forgivingly. The count's servant assured them that his master had left the city for Monza. 'Is Medole a coward?' cried Luciano, almost in the servant's hearing. The fleeing of so important a man looked vile, now that they were sharpened by new eagerness. Forthwith they were off to Agostino, believing that he would know the truth. They found him in bed. 'Well, and what?' said Agostino, replying to their laughter. 'I am old; too old to stride across a day and night, like you giants of youth. I take my rest when I can, for I must have it.'

'But, you know, O conscript father,' said Carlo, willing to fall a little into his mood, 'you know that nothing will be done to-night.'

'Do I know so much?' Agostino murmured at full length.

'Do you know that the Chief is in the city?' said Luciano.

'A man who is lying in bed knows this,' returned Agostino, 'that he knows less than those who are up, though what he does know he perhaps digests better. 'Tis you who are the fountains, my boys, while I am the pool into which you play. Say on.'

They spoke of the rumour. He smiled at it. They saw at once that the rumour was false, for the Chief trusted Agostino.

'Proceed to Barto, the mole,' he said, 'Barto the miner; he is the father of daylight in the city: of the daylight of knowledge, you understand, for which men must dig deep. Proceed to him;—if you can find him.'

But Carlo brought flame into Agostino's eyes.

'The accursed beast! he has pinned the black butterfly to the signorina's dress.'

Agostino rose on his elbow. He gazed at them. 'We are followers of a blind mole,' he uttered with an inner voices while still gazing wrathfully, and then burst out in grief, '"Patria o mea creatrix, patria o mea genetrix!"'

'The signorina takes none of his warnings, nor do we. She escaped a plot last night, and to-night she sings.'

'She must not,' said Agostino imperiously.

'She does.'

'I must stop that.' Agostino jumped out of bed.

The young men beset him with entreaties to leave the option to her.

'Fools!' he cried, plunging a rageing leg into his garments. 'Here, Iris! Mercury! fly to Jupiter and say we are all old men and boys in Italy, and are ready to accept a few middleaged mortals as Gods, if they will come and help us. Young fools! Do you know that when you conspire you are in harness, and yoke-fellows, every one?'

'Yoked to that Barto Rizzo!'

'Yes; and the worse horse of the two. Listen, you pair of Nuremberg puppet-heads! If the Chief were here, I would lie still in my bed. Medole has stopped the outbreak. Right or wrong, he moves a mass; we are subordinates — particles. The Chief can't be everywhere. Milan is too hot for him. Two men are here, concealed — Rinaldo and Angelo Guidascarpi. The rumour springs from that. They have slain Count Paul Lenkenstein, and rushed to old Milan for work, with the blood on their swords. Oh, the tragedy! — when I have time to write it. Let me now go to my girl, to my daughter! The blood of the Lenkenstein must rust on the steel. Angelo slew him: Rinaldo gave him the cross to kiss. You shall have the whole story by-and-by; but this will be a lesson to Germans not to court our Italian damsels. Lift not that curtain, you Pannonian burglars! Much do we pardon; but bow and viol meet not, save that they be of one wood; especially not when signor bow is from yonderside the Rhoetian Alps, and donzella Viol is a growth of warm Lombardy. Witness to it, Angelo and Rinaldo

Guidascarpi! bravo! You boys there—you stand like two Tyrolese salad-spoons! I say that my girl, my daughter, shall never help to fire blank shot. I sent my paternal commands to her yesterday evening. Does the wanton disobey her father and look up to a pair of rocket-headed rascals like you? Apes! if she sings that song to-night, the ear of Italy will be deaf to her for ever after. There's no engine to stir to-night; all the locks are on it; she will send half-a-dozen milkings like you to perdition, and there will be a circle of black blood about her name in the traditions of the insurrection—do you hear? Have I cherished her for that purpose? to have her dedicated to a brawl!'

Agostino fumed up and down the room in a confusion of apparel, savouring his epithets and imaginative peeps while he stormed, to get a relish out of something, as beseems the poetic temperament. The youths were silenced by him; Carlo gladly.

'Troop!' said the old man, affecting to contrast his attire with theirs; 'two graces and a satyr never yet went together, and we'll not frighten the classic Government of Milan. I go out alone. No, Signor Luciano, I am not sworn to Count Medole. I see your sneer contain it. Ah! what a thing is hurry to a mind like mine. It tears up the trees by the roots, floods the land, darkens utterly my poor quiet universe. I was composing a pastoral when you came in. Observe what you have done with my "Lovely Age of Gold!"'

Agostino's transfigurement from lymphatic poet to fiery man of action, lasted till his breath was short, when the necessity for taking a deep draught of air induced him to fall back upon his idle irony. 'Heads, you illustrious young gentlemen!—heads, not legs and arms, move a conspiracy. Now, you—think what you will of it—are only legs and arms in this business. And if you are insubordinate, you present the shocking fabular spirit of the members of the body in revolt; which is not the revolt we desire to see. I go to my daughter immediately, and we shall all have a fat sleep for a week, while the Tedeschi hunt and stew and exhaust their naughty suspicions. Do you know that the Pope's Mouth is closed? We made it tell a big lie before it shut tight on its teeth—a bad omen, I admit; but the idea was rapturously neat. Barto, the sinner —be sure I throttle him for putting that blot on my swan; only, not yet, not yet: he's a blind mole, a mad patriot; but, as I say, our beast Barto drew an Austrian to the Mouth last night, and led the dog to take a letter out of it, detailing the whole plot of tonight, and how men will be stationed at the vicolo here, ready to burst out on the Corso, and at the vicolo there, and elsewhere, all over the city, carrying fire and sword; a systematic map of the plot. It was addressed to Count Serabiglione—my boys! my boys! what do you think of it? Bravo! though Barto is a deadly beast if he—'Agostino paused. 'Yes, he went too far! too far!'

'Has he only gone too far, do you say?'

Carlo spoke sternly. His elder was provoked enough by his deadness of enthusiasm, and that the boy should dare to stalk on a bare egoistical lover's sentiment to be critical of him, Agostino, struck him as monstrous. With the treachery of controlled rage, Agostino drew near him, and whispered some sentences in his ear.

Agostino then called him his good Spartan boy for keeping brave countenance. 'Wait till you comprehend women philosophically. All's trouble with them till then. At La Scala tonight, my sons! We have rehearsed the fiasco; the Tedeschi perform it. Off with you, that I may go out alone!'

He seemed to think it an indubitable matter that he would find Vittoria and bend her will.

Agostino had betrayed his weakness to the young men, who read him with the keen eyes of a particular disapprobation. He delighted in the dark web of intrigue, and believed himself to be no ordinary weaver of that sunless work. It captured his imagination, filling his pride with a mounting gas. Thus he had become allied to Medole on the one hand, and to Barto Rizzo on the other. The young men read him shrewdly, but speaking was useless.

Before Carlo parted from Luciano, he told him the burden of the whisper, which had confirmed what he had heard on the Piazzi d'Armi. It was this: Barto Rizzo, aware that Lieutenant Pierson was the bearer of despatches from the Archduke in Milan to the marshal, then in Verona, had followed, and by extraordinary effort reached Verona in advance; had there tricked and waylaid him, and obtained, instead of despatches, a letter of recent date, addressed to him by Vittoria, which compromised the insurrectionary project.

'If that's the case, my Carlo!' said his friend, and shrugged, and spoke in a very worldly fashion of the fair sex.

Carlo shook him off. For the rest of the day he was alone, shut up with his journalistic pen. The pen traversed seas and continents like an old hack to whom his master has thrown the reins. Apart from the desperate perturbation of his soul, he thought of the Guidascarpi, whom he knew, and was allied to, and of the Lenkensteins, whom he knew likewise, or had known in the days when Giacomo Piaveni lived, and Bianca von Lenkenstein, Laura's sister, visited among the people of her country. Countess Anna and Countess Lena von Lenkenstein were the German beauties of Milan, lively little women, and sweet. Between himself and Countess Lena there had been tender dealings about the age when sweetmeats have lost their attraction, and the charm has to be supplied. She was rich, passionate for Austria, romantic concerning Italy, a vixen in temper, but with a pearly light about her temples that kept her picture in his memory. And besides, during those days when women are bountiful to us as Goddesses, give they never so little, she had deigned to fondle hands with him; had set the universe rocking with a visible heave of her bosom; jingled all the keys of mystery; and had once (as to embalm herself in his recollection), once had surrendered her lips to him. Countess Lena would have espoused Ammiani, believing in her power to make an Austrian out of such Italian material. The Piaveni revolt had stopped that and all their intercourse by the division of the White Hand, as it was called; otherwise, the hand of the corpse. Ammiani had known also Count Paul von Lenkenstein. To his mind, death did not mean much, however pleasant life might be: his father and his friend had gone to it gaily; and he himself stood ready for the summons: but the contemplation of a domestic judicial execution, which the Guidascarpi seemed to have done upon Count Paul, affrighted him, and put an end to his temporary capacity for labour. He felt as if a spent shot were striking on his ribs; it was the unknown sensation of fear. Changeing, it became pity. 'Horrible deaths these Austrians die!' he said.

For a while he regarded their lot as the hardest. A shaft of sunlight like blazing brass warned him that the day dropped. He sent to his mother's stables, and rode at a gallop round Milan, dining alone in one of the common hotel gardens, where he was a stranger. A man may have good nerve to face the scene which he is certain will be enacted, who shrinks from an hour that is suspended in doubt. He was aware of the pallor and chill of his looks, and it was no marvel to him when two sbirri in mufti, foreign to Milan, set their eyes on him as they passed by to a vacant table on the farther side of the pattering gold-fish pool, where he sat. He divined that they might be in pursuit of the Guidascarpi, and alive to read a troubled visage. 'Yet neither Rinaldo nor Angelo would look as I do now,' he thought, perceiving that these men were judging by such signs, and had their ideas. Democrat as he imagined himself to be, he despised with a nobleman's contempt creatures who were so dead to the character of men of birth as to suppose that they were pale and remorseful after dealing a righteous blow, and that they trembled! Ammiani looked at his hand: no force of his will could arrest its palsy. The Guidascarpi were sons of Bologna. The stupidity of Italian sbirri is proverbial, or a Milanese cavalier would have been astonished to conceive himself mistaken for a Bolognese. He beckoned to the waiter, and said, 'Tell me what place has bred those two fellows on the other side of the fountain.' After a side-glance of scrutiny, the reply was, 'Neapolitans.' The waiter was ready to make an additional remark, but Ammiani nodded and communed with a toothpick. He was sure that those Neapolitans were recruits of the Bolognese Polizia; on the track of the Guidascarpi, possibly. As he was not unlike Angelo Guidascarpi in figure, he became uneasy lest they should blunder 'twixt him and La Scala; and the notion of any human power stopping him short of that destination, made Ammiani's hand perfectly firm. He drew on his gloves, and named the place whither he was going, aloud. 'Excellency,' said the waiter, while taking up and pretending to reckon the money for the bill: 'they have asked me whether there are two Counts Ammiani in Milan.' Carlo's eyebrows started. 'Can they be after me?' he thought, and said: 'Certainly; there is twice anything in this world, and Milan is the epitome of it.'

Acting a part gave him Agostino's catching manner of speech. The waiter, who knew him now, took this for an order to say 'Yes.' He had evidently a respect for Ammiani's name: Carlo supposed that he was one of Milan's fighting men. A sort of answer leading to 'Yes' by a circuit and the assistance of the hearer, was conveyed to the, sbirri. They were true Neapolitans quick to suspect, irresolute upon their suspicions. He was soon aware that they were not to be feared more than are the general race of bunglers, whom the Gods sometimes strangely favour. They perplexed him: for why were they after him? and what had made them ask whether he had a brother? He was followed, but not molested, on his way to La Scala.

Ammiani's heart was in full play as he looked at the curtain of the stage. The Night of the Fifteenth had come. For the first few moments his strong excitement fronting the curtain, amid a great host of hearts thumping and quivering up in the smaller measures like his own, together with the predisposing belief that this was to be a night of events, stopped his consciousness that all had been thwarted; that there was nothing but plot, plot, counterplot and tangle, disunion, silly subtlety, jealousy, vanity, a direful congregation of antagonistic elements; threads all loose, tongues wagging, pressure here, pressure there, like an uncertain rage in the entrails of the undirected earth, and no master hand on the spot to fuse and point the intense distracted forces.

The curtain, therefore, hung like any common opera-screen; big only with the fate of the new prima donna. He was robbed even of the certainty that Vittoria would appear. From the blank aspect of the curtain he turned to the house, which was crowding fast, and was not like listless Milan about to criticize an untried voice. The commonly empty boxes of the aristocracy were full of occupants, and for a wonder the white uniforms were not in excess, though they were to be seen. The first person whom Ammiani met was Agostino, who spoke gruffly. Vittoria had been invisible to him. Neither the maestro, nor the impresario, nor the waiting-woman had heard of her. Uncertainty was behind the curtain, as well as in front; but in front it was the uncertainty which is tipped with expectation, hushing the usual noisy chatter, and setting a daylight of eyes forward. Ammiani spied about the house, and caught sight of Laura Piaveni with Colonel Corte by her side. The Lenkensteins were in the Archduke's box. Antonio-Pericles, and the English lady and Captain Gambier, were next to them. The appearance of a white uniform in his mother's box over the stage caused Ammiani to shut up his glass. He was making his way thither for the purpose of commencing the hostilities of the night, when Countess Ammiani entered the lobby, and took her son's arm with a grave face and a trembling touch.

CHAPTER XIX
THE PRIMA DONNA

'Whover is in my box is my guest,' said the countess, adding a convulsive imperative pressure on Carlo's arm, to aid the meaning of her deep underbreath. She was a woman who rarely exacted obedience, and she was spontaneously obeyed. No questions could be put, no explanations given in the crash, and they threaded on amid numerous greetings in a place where Milanese society had habitually ceased to gather, and found itself now in assembly with unconcealed sensations of strangeness. A card lay on the table of the countess's private retiring-room: it bore the name of General Pierson. She threw off her black lace scarf. 'Angelo Guidascarpi is in Milan,' she said. 'He has killed one of the Lenkensteins, sword to sword. He came to me an hour after you left; the sbirri were on his track; he passed for my son. He is now under the charge of Barto Rizzo, disguised; probably in this house. His brother is in the city. Keep the cowl on your head as long as possible; if these hounds see and identify you, there will be mischief.' She said no more, satisfied that she was understood, but opening the door of the box, passed in, and returned a stately acknowledgement of the salutations of two military officers. Carlo likewise bent his head to them; it was like bending his knee, for in the younger of the two intruders he recognized Lieutenant Pierson. The countess accepted a vacated seat; the cavity of her ear accepted the General's apologies. He informed her that he deeply regretted the intrusion; he was under orders to be present at the opera, and to be as near the stage as possible, the countess's box being designated. Her face had the unalterable composure of a painted head upon an old canvas. The General persisted in tendering excuses. She replied, 'It is best, when one is too weak to resist, to submit to an outrage quietly.' General Pierson at once took the position assigned to him; it was not an agreeable one. Between Carlo and the lieutenant no attempt at conversation was made.

The General addressed his nephew in English. 'Did you see the girl behind the scenes, Wilfrid?'

The answer was 'No.'

'Pericles has her fast shut up in the Tyrol: the best habitat for her if she objects to a whipping. Did you see Irma?'

'No; she has disappeared too.'

'Then I suppose we must make up our minds to an opera without head or tail. As Pat said of the sack of potatoes, "'twould be a mighty fine beast if it had them."'

The officers had taken refuge in their opera-glasses, and spoke while gazing round the house.

'If neither this girl nor Irma is going to appear, there is no positive necessity for my presence here,' said the General, reduced to excuse himself to himself. 'I'll sit through the first scene and then beat a retreat. I might be off at once; the affair looks harmless enough only, you know, when there's nothing to see, you must report that you have seen it, or your superiors are not satisfied.'

The lieutenant was less able to cover the irksomeness of his situation with easy talk. His glance rested on Countess Len a von Lenkenstein, a quick motion of whose hand made him say that he should go over to her.

'Very well,' said the General; 'be careful that you give no hint of this horrible business. They will hear of it when they get home: time enough!'

Lieutenant Pierson touched at his sister's box on the way. She was very excited, asked innumerable things, — whether there was danger? whether he had a whole regiment at hand to protect peaceable persons? 'Otherwise,' she said, 'I shall not be able to keep that man (her husband) in Italy another week. He refused to stir out to-night, though we know that nothing can happen. Your prima donna celestissima is out of harm's way.'

'Oh, she is safe, — ze minx'; cried Antonio-Pericles, laughing and saluting the Duchess of Graatli, who presented herself at the front of her box. Major de Pyrmont was behind her, and it delighted the Greek to point them out to the English lady, with a simple intimation of the character of their relationship, at which her curls shook sadly.

'Pardon, madame,' said Pericles. 'In Italy, a husband away, ze friend takes title: it is no more.'

'It is very disgraceful,' she said.

'Ze morales, madame, suit ze sun.'

Captain Gambier left the box with Wilfrid, expressing in one sentence his desire to fling Pericles over to the pit, and in another his belief that an English friend, named Merthyr Powys, was in the house.

'He won't be in the city four-and-twenty hours,' said Wilfrid.

'Well; you'll keep your tongue silent.'

'By heavens! Gambier, if you knew the insults we have to submit to! The temper of angels couldn't stand it. I'm sorry enough for these fellows, with their confounded country, but it's desperate work to be civil to them; upon my honour, it is! I wish they would stand up and let us have it over. We have to bear more from the women than the men.'

'I leave you to cool,' said Gambier.

The delayed absence of the maestro from his post at the head of the orchestra, where the musicians sat awaiting him, seemed to confirm a rumour that was now circling among the audience, warning all to prepare for a disappointment. His baton was brought in and laid on the book of the new overture. When at last he was seen bearing onward through the music-stands, a low murmur ran round. Rocco paid no heed to it. His demeanour produced such satisfaction in the breast of Antonio-Pericles that he rose, and was guilty of the barbarism of clapping his hands. Meeting Ammiani in the lobby, he said, 'Come, my good friend, you shall help me to pull Irma through to-night. She is vinegar—we will mix her with oil. It is only for to-night, to save that poor Rocco's opera.'

'Irma!' said Ammiani; 'she is by this time in Tyrol. Your Irma will have some difficulty in showing herself here within sixty hours.'

'How!' cried Pericles, amazed, and plucking after Carlo to stop him. 'I bet you—'

'How much?'

'I bet you a thousand florins you do not see la Vittoria to-night.'

'Good. I bet you a thousand florins you do not see Irma.'

'No Vittoria, I say!'

'And I say, no Lazzeruola!'

Agostino, who was pacing the lobby, sent Pericles distraught with the same tale of the rape of Irma. He rushed to Signora Piaveni's box and heard it repeated. There he beheld, sitting in the background, an old English acquaintance, with whom Captain Gambier was conversing.

'My dear Powys, you have come all the way from England to see your favourite's first night. You will be shocked, sir. She has neglected her Art. She is exiled, banished, sent away to study and to compose her mind.'

'I think you are mistaken,' said Laura. 'You will see her almost immediately.'

'Signora, pardon me; do I not know best?'

'You may have contrived badly.'

Pericles blinked and gnawed his moustache as if it were food for patience.

'I would wager a milliard of francs,' he muttered. With absolute pathos he related to Mr. Powys the aberrations of the divinely-gifted voice, the wreck which Vittoria strove to become, and from which he alone was striving to rescue her. He used abundant illustrations, coarse and quaint, and was half hysterical; flashing a white fist and thumping the long projection of his knee with a wolfish aspect. His grotesque sincerity was little short of the shedding of tears.

'And your sister, my dear Powys?' he asked, as one returning to the consideration of shadows.

'My sister accompanies me, but not to the opera.'

'For another campaign—hein?'

'To winter in Italy, at all events.'

Carlo Ammiani entered and embraced Merthyr Powys warmly. The Englishman was at home among Italians: Pericles, feeling that he was not so, and regarding them all as a community of fever-patients without hospital, retired. To his mind it was the vilest treason, the grossest selfishness, to conspire or to wink at the sacrifice of a voice like Vittoria's to such a temporal matter as this, which they called patriotism. He looked on it as one might look on the Hindoo drama of a Suttee. He saw in it just that stupid action of a whole body of fanatics combined to precipitate the devotion of a precious thing to extinction. And worse; for life was common, and women and Hindoo widows were common; but a Vittorian voice was but one in a generation—in a cycle of years. The religious belief of the connoisseur extended to the devout conception that her voice was a spiritual endowment, the casting of which priceless jewel into the bloody ditch of patriots was far more tragic and lamentable than any disastrous concourse of dedicated lives. He shook the lobby with his tread, thinking of the great night this might have been but for Vittoria's madness. The overture was coming to an end. By tightening his arms across his chest he gained some outward composure, and fixed his eyes upon the stage.

While sitting with Laura Piaveni and Merthyr Powys, Ammiani saw the apparition of Captain Weisspriess in his mother's box. He forgot her injunction, and hurried to her side, leaving the doors open. His passion of anger spurned her admonishing grasp of his arm, and with his glove he smote the Austrian officer on the face. Weisspriess plucked his sword out; the house rose; there was a moment like that of a wild beast's show of teeth. It passed: Captain Weisspriess withdrew in obedience to General Pierson's command. The latter wrote on a slip of paper that two pieces of artillery should be placed in position, and a squad of men about the doors: he handed it out to Weisspriess.

'I hope,' the General said to Carlo, 'we shall be able to arrange things for you without the interposition of the authorities.'

Carlo rejoined, 'General, he has the blood of our family on his hands. I am ready.'

The General bowed. He glanced at the countess for a sign of maternal weakness, saw none, and understood that a duel was down in the morrow's bill of entertainments, as well as a riot possibly before dawn. The house had revealed its temper in that short outburst, as a quivering of quick lightning-flame betrays the forehead of the storm.

Countess Ammiani bade her son make fast the outer door. Her sedate energies could barely control her agitation. In helping Angelo Guidascarpi to evade the law, she had imperilled her son and herself. Many of the Bolognese sbirri were in pursuit of Angelo. Some knew his person; some did not; but if those two before whom she had identified Angelo as being her son Carlo chanced now to be in the house, and to have seen him, and heard his name, the risks were great and various.

'Do you know that handsome young Count Ammiani?' Countess Lena said to Wilfrid. 'Perhaps you do not think him handsome? He was for a short time a play-fellow of mine. He is more passionate than I am, and that does not say a little; I warn you! Look how excited he is. No wonder. He is — everybody knows it — he is la Vittoria's lover.'

Countess Lena uttered that sentence in Italian. The soft tongue sent it like a coiling serpent through Wilfrid's veins. In English or in German it would not have possessed the deadly meaning.

She may have done it purposely, for she and her sister Countess Anna studied his face. The lifting of the curtain drew all eyes to the stage.

Rocco Ricci's baton struck for the opening of one of his spirited choruses; a chorus of villagers, who sing to the burden that Happiness, the aim of all humanity, has promised to visit the earth this day, that she may witness the union of the noble lovers, Camillo and Camilla. Then a shepherd sings a verse, with his hand stretched out to the impending castle. There lives Count Orso: will he permit their festivities to pass undisturbed? The puling voice is crushed by the chorus, which protests that the heavens are above Count Orso. But another villager tells of Orso's power, and hints at his misdeeds. The chorus rises in reply, warning all that Count Orso has ears wherever three are congregated; the villagers break apart and eye one another distrustfully, reuniting to the song of Happiness before they disperse. Camillo enters solus. Montini, as Camillo, enjoyed a warm reception; but as he advanced to deliver his canzone, it was seen that he and Rocco interchanged glances of desperate resignation. Camillo has had love passages with Michiella, Count Orso's daughter, and does not hesitate to declare that he dreads her. The orphan Camilla, who has been reared in yonder castle with her, as her sister, is in danger during all these last minutes which still retain her from his arms.

'If I should never see her — I who, like a poor ghost upon the shores of the dead river, have been flattered with the thought that she would fall upon my breast like a ray of the light of Elysium — if I should never see her more!' The famous tenore threw his whole force into that outcry of projected despair, and the house was moved by it: there were many in the house who shared his apprehension of a foul mischance.

Thenceforward the opera and the Italian audience were as one. All that was uttered had a meaning, and was sympathetically translated. Camilla they perceived to be a grave burlesque with a core to it. The quick- witted Italians caught up the interpretation in a flash. 'Count Orso' Austria; 'Michiella' is Austria's spirit of intrigue; 'Camillo' is indolent Italy, amorous Italy, Italy aimless; 'Camilla' is YOUNG ITALY!

Their eagerness for sight of Vittoria was now red-hot, and when Camillo exclaimed 'She comes!' many rose from their seats.

A scrap of paper was handed to Antonio-Pericles from Captain Weisspriess, saying briefly that he had found Irma in the carriage instead of the little 'v,' thanked him for the joke, and had brought her back. Pericles was therefore not surprised when Irma, as Michiella, came on, breathless, and looking in an excitement of anger; he knew that he had been tricked.

Between Camillo and Michiella a scene of some vivacity ensued— reproaches, threats of calamity, offers of returning endearment upon her part; a display of courtly scorn upon his. Irma made her voice claw at her quondam lover very finely; it was a voice with claws, that entered the hearing sharp-edged, and left it plucking at its repose. She was applauded relishingly when, after vainly wooing him, she turned aside and said—

'What change is this in one who like a reed
    Bent to my twisting hands? Does he recoil?
    Is this the hound whom I have used to feed
    With sops of vinegar and sops of oil?'

Michiella's further communications to the audience make it known that she has allowed the progress toward the ceremonies of espousal between Camillo and Camilla, in order, at the last moment, to show her power over the youth and to plunge the detested Camilla into shame and wretchedness.

Camillo retires: Count Orso appears. There is a duet between father and daughter: she confesses her passion for Camillo, and entreats her father to stop the ceremony; and here the justice of the feelings of Italians, even in their heat of blood, was noteworthy. Count Orso says that he would willingly gratify his daughter, as it would gratify himself, but that he must respect the law. 'The law is of your own making,' says Michiella. 'Then, the more must I respect it,' Count Orso replies.

The audience gave Austria credit for that much in a short murmur.

Michiella's aside, 'Till anger seizes him I wait!' created laughter; it came in contrast with an extraordinary pomposity of self-satisfaction exhibited by Count Orso—the flower-faced, tun-bellied basso, Lebruno. It was irresistible. He stood swollen out like a morning cock. To make it further telling, he took off his yellow bonnet with a black-gloved hand, and thumped the significant colours prominently on his immense chest—an idea, not of Agostino's, but Lebruno's own; and Agostino cursed with fury. Both he and Rocco knew that their joint labour would probably have only one night's display of existence in the Austrian dominions, but they grudged to Lebruno the chief merit of despatching it to the Shades.

The villagers are heard approaching. 'My father!' cries Michiella, distractedly; 'the hour is near: it will be death to your daughter! Imprison Camillo: I can bring twenty witnesses to prove that he has sworn you are illegally the lord of this country. You will rue the marriage. Do as you once did. Be bold in time. The arrow-head is on the string- cut the string!'

'As I once did?' replies Orso with frown terrific, like a black crest. He turns broadly and receives the chorus of countrymen in paternal fashion—an admirably acted bit of grave burlesque.

By this time the German portion of the audience had, by one or other of the senses, dimly divined that the opera was a shadow of something concealed—thanks to the buffo-basso Lebruno. Doubtless they would have seen this before, but that the Austrian censorship had seemed so absolute a safeguard.

'My children! all are my children in this my gladsome realm!' Count Orso says, and marches forth, after receiving the compliment of a choric song in honour of his paternal government. Michiella follows him.

Then came the deep suspension of breath. For, as upon the midnight you count bell-note after bell-note of the toiling hour, and know not in the darkness whether there shall be one beyond it, so that you hang over an abysm until Twelve is sounded, audience and actors gazed with equal expectation at the path winding round from the castle, waiting for the voice of the new prima donna.

'Mia madre!' It issued tremblingly faint. None could say who was to appear.

Rocco Ricci struck twice with his baton, flung a radiant glance across his shoulders for all friends, and there was joy in the house. Vittoria stood before them.